# THE GIRL
## *who swam with*
# THE FISH

## AN ATHABASCAN LEGEND

Retold by

### MICHELLE RENNER

———

Illustrated by

### CHRISTINE COX

### ALASKA NORTHWEST BOOKS™

Anchorage • Seattle • Portland

*For my mom and dad, with love*

Library of Congress Cataloging-in-Publication Data

Renner, Michelle, 1954-
    The girl who swam with the fish / retold by Michelle Renner ;
illustrated by Christine Cox.
        p.    cm.
    ISBN 0-88240-442-3
    1. Athapascan Indians—Folklore.  2. Legends—North America.
I.  Cox, Christine, 1957-  ill.  II. Title.
E99. A86K78  1995
398. 2'089972—dc20                          94-13763
                                            CIP
                                            AC

Editor: Marlene Blessing
Designer: Constance Bollen


**Alaska Northwest Books™**
An imprint of Graphic Arts Center Publishing Company
Editorial office: 2208 NW Market Street, Suite 300, Seattle, WA 98107
Catalog and order dept.: P.O. Box 10306, Portland, OR 97210
    800-452-3032


Printed on acid-free paper in Korea

## A WORD ABOUT
## THE SOURCE OF THIS STORY

*The Girl Who Swam with the Fish* is a retelling of an Athabascan story narrated by the late Miska Deaphon, an elder from the Alaskan village of Nikolai. Nikolai is located on the South Fork of the Kuskokwim River, near the town of McGrath. This and other stories were originally translated and published in a collection entitled *Nikolai Hwch'ihwzoya',* produced by the National Bilingual Materials Development Center at the University of Alaska, Anchorage.

A deep respect for salmon and other animals that provide sustenance for the Native people of Alaska is a common theme in their traditional myths and legends. In this story, the returning salmon are treated as honored guests. Salmon are a vital food source, and their annual homecoming helps to ensure the continuance of an important cultural lifestyle.

*The Girl Who Swam with the Fish* reminds us all of the sacredness of the natural world, its creatures and its cycles.

Long ago, during the moon when the leaves turn green, a young girl stood on the steep bank of a clear river, waiting for the fish to return. At this time of year, the fierce, fiery sun hung in the sky all day and all night, and mosquitoes buzzed and hummed everywhere.

Still, despite the heat and the biting insects, she waited. She waited for the fish to return.

Farther up the river, the girl's father and brother lashed together long poles of spruce to make the drying racks. Soon, she thought, fresh salmon would hang from the racks. Preserved by the sun and flavored over smoky fires, the fish would help them survive during wintertime.

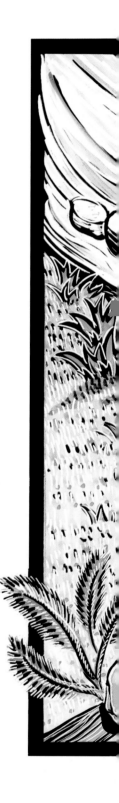

Often during the past winter, the girl and her family had been hungry. Now, gazing out at the water, she hoped the fish would honor her people by returning to the river.

Though dressed in her summer parka of tanned moose hide, the girl felt uncomfortably warm. Behind her, a stand of white birch trees offered shade, but she chose to stay on the sunny riverbank.

The girl wondered what it would be like to be a fish, to glide through cool waves, hearing only the silence of the water. Where did fish travel? What sights did they see?

As she thought of these things, she heard a sudden, loud splash in the river. Her heart beat fast when she

peered over the edge of the bank.

They were here! The majestic king salmon had
returned! Mighty fins and tails churned the water where
the salmon swam against the current to the place of
their birth.

The girl marveled at the sight and longed for a closer look.  Gripping some willows that grew along the bank, she began to climb down to the river.  But her foot slipped on the loose gravel.  Before she could cry out, she had tumbled into the water.

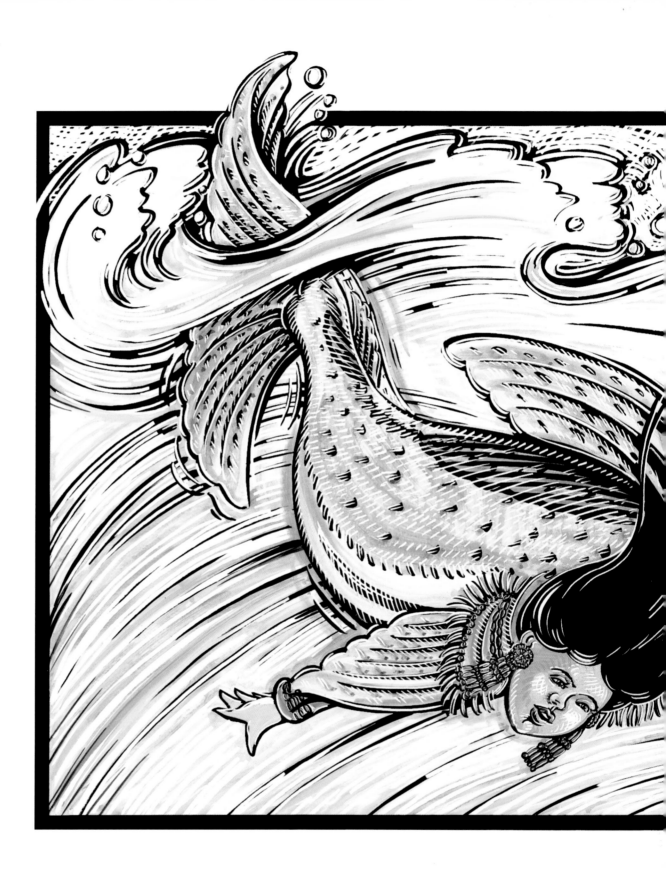

The weight of her wet clothing pulled the girl under, and her long, dark hair swirled in the river's current. Frightened, she twisted and struggled, when suddenly she began to swim.

How can I be swimming? she wondered, since she did not know how to swim. Then, looking down at herself, she saw she had changed into a salmon!

In the days that followed, the girl lived in the river.
She saw the big salmon spawn and she swam with the
newly hatched little ones.

At times, she watched her own family on the shore, and
saw the sadness in their faces. She tried to call to them.

But, of course, they could not hear her.

When the young salmon were ready to swim to the sea, the girl looked back toward her family's fish camp. Soon her parents and her brother would leave to hunt caribou. But now she was a fish and could not follow them.

For days and months, she traveled down the river with the fish. The water became muddy until, at last, they came to the place where the river met the sea.

Here, she saw creatures she had never seen before. Sometimes she saw big fish eating little fish. But none of them ever bothered her. During her first year at the ocean's edge, the girl's own fish body grew bigger.

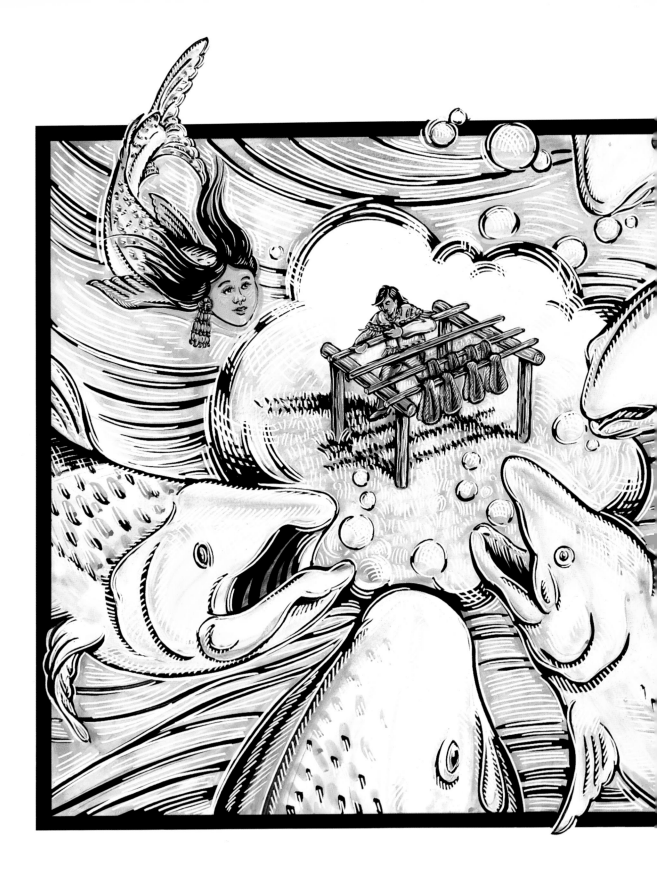

When spring came, the fish gathered to speak of how they wished to be treated by the people of the river.

For example, the people did not always clean the drying racks before they hung up the fish. The fish agreed they would return only to the people who cleaned their racks every year.

The girl listened to the fish and remembered what they said.

As another year passed, the girl's fish body grew even bigger.  Again, the fish gathered in the ocean.  This time the fish agreed to return only to the people who kept their cutting knives sharp.

The girl listened and remembered.

Over time, the girl learned more about how the fish wished to be treated. If fish meat was drying on the racks and it began to rain, the people must turn the fish over so the shiny, waterproof scales on the other side would protect the meat from getting wet and rotting.

The girl listened to all these things and remembered.

Finally, the girl grew big enough to journey back
to the river. She swam for many days until she
saw her family's camp.

She was so happy to see her parents, she leaped out of

the water and onto the shore, where she became a girl
again.  Joyfully, they rushed to her and asked where she
had been all these years.  "I fell in the river and became a
king salmon," she answered.  "And I swam to the ocean."

Then she told them what she had learned from the fish about how they wished to be treated when they returned.

From that time on, the girl's family always cleaned their drying racks and sharpened their cutting knives. When rain came, someone made sure the silver, shiny sides of the fish were turned up.

And the fish always returned to the family's camp by the river.

The people decided to call the girl *The Girl Who Swam with the Fish*. She lived happily for a very long time. And each summer, she would go to the river to wait and watch.

She waited for the fish to return.